The Lost Diary of Robin Hood's Money Man

The Lost Diary of Robin Hood's Money Man

Found by Steve Barlow and Steve Skidmore
Illustrated by George Hollingworth

Collins

An imprint of HarperCollins*Publishers*

First published in Great Britain by Collins in 1999

Collins is an imprint of HarperCollins*Publishers* Ltd,
77-85 Fulham Palace Road, Hammersmith, London W6 8JB

The HarperCollins website address is www.**fire**and**water**.com

ISBN 0 00 694591 0

Printed and bound in Great Britain by
Caledonian International Book Manufacturing Ltd, Glasgow, G64

MESSAGE TO READERS

Many people believe that the famous English outlaw, Robin Hood, is merely a legendary figure. They argue that he only ever existed as a character in stories, plays and songs.

However, this recently discovered Lost Diary proves beyond doubt that Robin Hood *did* exist.

The diary is written by Leonard du Somoney, Robin Hood's financial advisor in Sherwood Forest (presumably his branch manager). It details how Robin Hood became an outlaw. It also provides records of the Third Crusade and inside views of Richard the Lionheart and his brother John.

This diary (like so many other Lost Diaries) was found by Barlow and Skidmore. They were truffle* hunting in Sherwood Forest with their pet pig, Percy, when the pig was drawn towards a giant oak tree. Instead of finding truffles, Percy dug up a pink pottery piggy bank. Breaking open the pig (the pottery one), Barlow and Skidmore discovered the following Lost Diary. There were also hundreds of pages of accounts, but the publishers thought these accounts were far too boring to put in this book (although the company accountant thought they were jolly interesting and made a riveting good read).

Instead, the editors chose the most interesting diary entries for publication. For the first time ever, we have a unique day-to-day record of life in Sherwood Forest, where Robin Hood and his band of outlaws robbed from the rich and gave to the poor. At last, we can see the Merry Man behind the legend.

---

* A truffle is an expensive fungus, not to be confused with trifle which is not found in forests except after very messy picnics.

I'm starting a new job tomorrow. As a Norman gentleman, and the son of a knight, I shouldn't have to work at all – but I'm the youngest son, so I don't get to inherit any money even if there was any, which there isn't because my dad has spent it all. So when I saw that Earl David of Huntingdon was looking for a Steward, I sent him my reference.

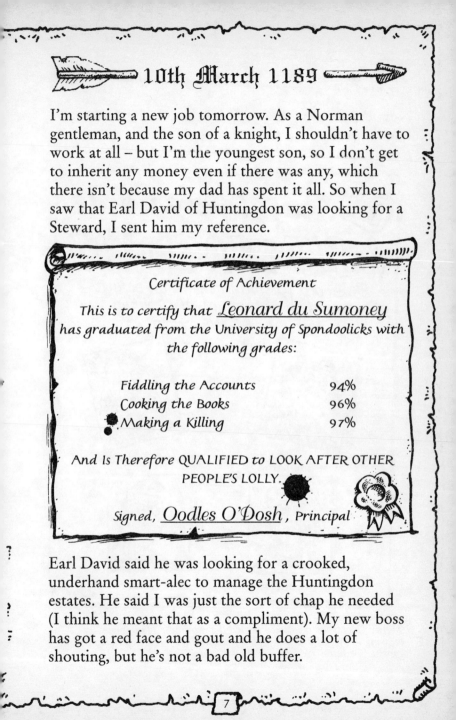

Certificate of Achievement

This is to certify that <u>Leonard du Sumoney</u> has graduated from the University of Spondoolicks with the following grades:

Fiddling the Accounts	94%
Cooking the Books	96%
Making a Killing	97%

And Is Therefore QUALIFIED to LOOK AFTER OTHER PEOPLE'S LOLLY.

Signed, <u>Oodles O'Dosh</u>, Principal

Earl David said he was looking for a crooked, underhand smart-alec to manage the Huntingdon estates. He said I was just the sort of chap he needed (I think he meant that as a compliment). My new boss has got a red face and gout and he does a lot of shouting, but he's not a bad old buffer.

Now I'm working for an earl, I thought I'd better catch up with what's been happening to the Royal Family.

Soap Opera Guide
The PLANTAGENETS*

Power and passion in the high-octane world of Norman royal politics!
~ STARRING ~

Dad and Mum

King Henry II of England, Count of Aquitaine

Eleanor of Aquitaine

The sons

Richard (Count of Poitou)

John

* Henry II's father, Geoffrey, earned the nickname Plantagenet by wearing a sprig of broom in his cap. In Latin, broom was called planta genista. Geddit?

The story so far:

King Henry, the Godfather of the Plantagenet clan, owns the largest kingdom in Europe, stretching from the Scottish borders to the Pyrenees. However, his power-mad sons want a piece of the action. Henry puts his boys on ice and gives them some castles to play with, but locks up his scheming wife Eleanor.

King Henry enters merger talks with the French King Philip Augustus, but his sons fall out. Henry joins John in a boardroom battle against Richard, but then they all get together to fight a hostile takeover bid by King Philip.

Meanwhile, over in the Holy Land*, the Muslims, under their leader Saladin, capture Jerusalem. King Philip, King Henry and Prince Richard patch up their differences and decide to go on a Crusade to recapture the Holy City.

But bitter rivalries surface again. Before they set off, Richard and Philip attack Henry. Wheeler-dealer John also moves in as the vultures gather.

Henry is forced to name Richard as his successor and dies in a very bad mood at Chinon on 6th July 1189.

This week's episode:
Richard – King of England!

Honestly, these soap operas – they're getting far too silly. Nothing like this happens in real life!**

* Land that today includes parts of Syria, the Lebanon, Palestine, Jordan and Israel.
** Yes it did!

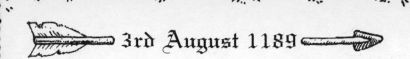

Earl David's nephew (he hasn't got any sons) has turned up from Locksley Manor. He's called Robert, and he's a right Hooray Henry. He keeps throwing bread rolls about at dinner and shouting "Ripping wheeze, what?" Upper class twit. I suppose he's harmless enough. He's getting married next summer to a girl called Marian. Actually, she calls herself "Mawian" as she can't pronounce her 'r's. She keeps saying things like, "Oh, Wobin, you are weally scwumptious!" She always calls him Wobin – sorry, I mean Robin – instead of Robert. It's a sort of pet name. She's got a laugh like a donkey with tummyache.

At least Marian has half a brain, which means that the two of them have got about three-quarters of a brain between them. I dread to think what their kids will be like.

10th August 1189

We're waiting for Richard to come over from France to be crowned King, now that his dad's dead. To pass the time, I've been helping young Robert update his *Big Boy's Kings of England Sticker Book*.

BIG BOY'S KINGS OF ENGLAND

Richard Plantagenet

Titles Count of Poitou, Duke of Normandy, Count of Aquitaine

Nickname Coeur de Lion (Lionheart)

Appearance Tall, red hair, strong, athletic

Education Educated at the court of Poitiers. Speaks several languages

Likes Fighting, arguing, fighting, writing poetry, fighting, music, fighting

Interesting facts

Born in Beaumont Palace, Oxford, on 8th September 1158

Been engaged to Alice, daughter of Louis VII of France, since 1169 (when he was twelve and she was eight)

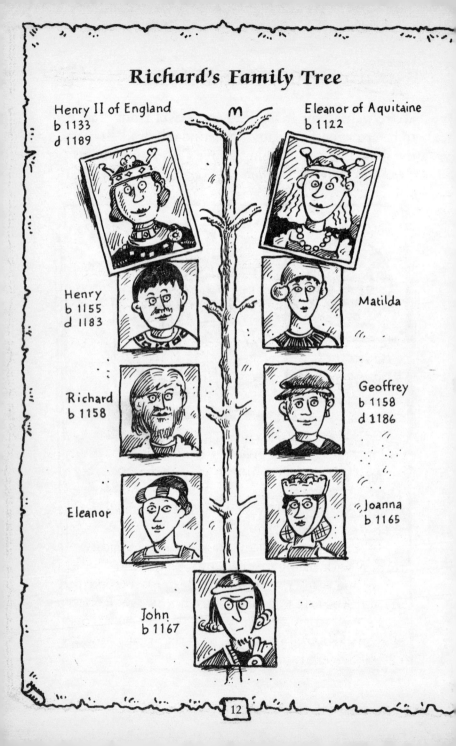

I've been arguing about politics with young master Robert.

His family originally came from Normandy in France (so did mine for that matter). We Normans arrived in England with William the Conqueror in 1066 and knocked seven barrels out of King Harold and his Saxons at the Battle of Hastings. Then we took most of the top jobs (and the land) from the Saxons. There are still a few rich Saxon families, but the real bossmen are French (thank goodness!). The Saxons are mainly tradespeople and peasants.

Robert owns Locksley Manor, and he's had several run-ins with the Sheriff of Nottingham. The Sheriff is a thug and a bully, and he treats his peasants like dirt. He and Robert don't exactly see eye to eye. Robert says it's a landowner's duty to look after his Saxon peasants and treat them with respect. That's how the Feudal System is meant to work.

The King →

Top banana, big cheese, numero uno. He owns all the land.

← Knights
These are called "Sir".
They can hold land.

Skilled workers
e.g. butchers potters, millers, stewards.

Noblemen →
(Lords, Barons and Earls)
The king gives them bits
of land to be in charge of

(and boss about the people
who live on that
bit of Land.)

**Officers of
the Crown**
(Like sheriffs)

These officers collect taxes
and work for the King
and the Nobles.

Peasants

Two main types - freemen and villeins:
• Free man can come and go as they please.
• Villeins are not allowed to leave the land
of a lord or a knight. They are
the property of
these nobles.
The nobles
can do
what they
like to these
peasants.

Maybe Robert's right – I can't be bothered to argue.
Money's money. Saxons earn it, I count it, Normans
spend it. End of story.

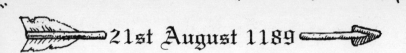

21st August 1189

Richard's back in England at last and Earl David has received his invitation (or rather command) to attend his coronation. The Earl has to hold a ceremonial sword for the King. He's taking me along to make sure young Robert doesn't embarrass us all (or get our bits cut off) by trying to play practical jokes or some other such nonsense.

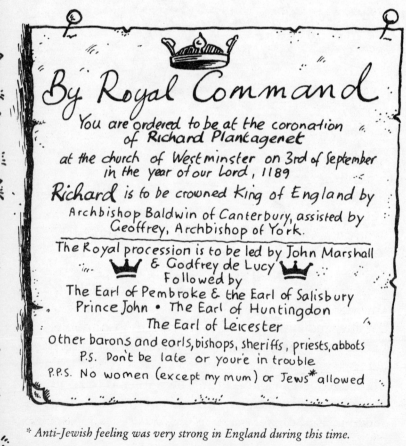

By Royal Command

You are ordered to be at the coronation of Richard Plantagenet
at the church of Westminster on 3rd of September in the year of our Lord, 1189

Richard is to be crowned King of England by Archbishop Baldwin of Canterbury, assisted by Geoffrey, Archbishop of York.

The Royal procession is to be led by John Marshall & Godfrey de Lucy
Followed by
The Earl of Pembroke & the Earl of Salisbury
Prince John • The Earl of Huntingdon
The Earl of Leicester
Other barons and earls, bishops, sheriffs, priests, abbots
P.S. Don't be late or you're in trouble
P.P.S. No women (except my mum) or Jews* allowed

* Anti-Jewish feeling was very strong in England during this time.

Richard deserves the throne
after what he had to go
through at the coronation.
Talk about embarrassing! He
had to stand at the front of
the church and get undressed
in front of everyone! He
stripped right down to his
undies. I'm surprised he
didn't catch a chill – it was
well draughty up the aisle.
Then he put on golden
sandals and had hot oil
poured all over him by a
priest. (Robert whispered to
me that the priest with the
hot oil was probably a fish

friar or a chip monk – I didn't laugh.) At last Richard
put on his clothes again, was crowned and we all
shouted hooray. Then we all trooped off for a big
feast. That's when the trouble started.

Some Jews tried to enter the banqueting hall to
present the King with a gift. However, they were
attacked by some of the guests. This set off the crowd
outside, and apparently they've run into London to
find as many Jews as they can. I'm not sure what they're
going to do, but it probably won't be very nice.*

* It wasn't. Hundreds of Jews were murdered and their houses ransacked
  and burnt.

Earl David, the silly old fool, is determined to join King Richard's Crusade to the Holy Land. My cousin, Basil Count de Money, is going too. He sent me a brochure.

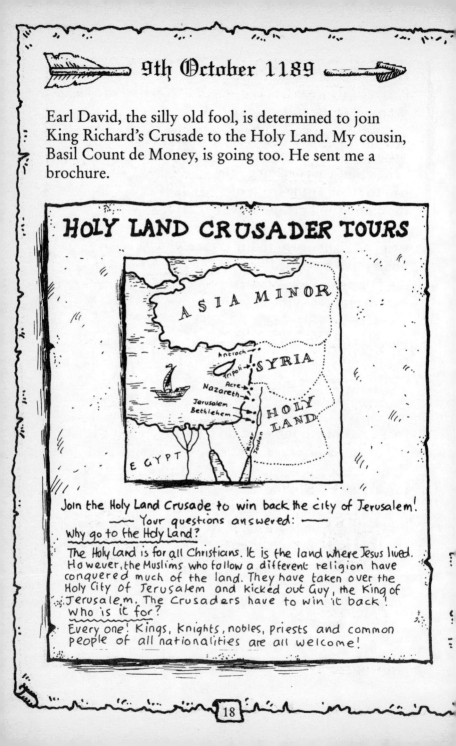

HOLY LAND CRUSADER TOURS

Join the Holy Land Crusade to win back the city of Jerusalem!

— Your questions answered: —

Why go to the Holy Land?

The Holy Land is for all Christians. It is the land where Jesus lived. However, the Muslims who follow a different religion have conquered much of the land. They have taken over the Holy City of Jerusalem and kicked out Guy, the King of Jerusalem. The Crusaders have to win it back!

Who is it for?

Everyone! Kings, knights, nobles, priests and common people of all nationalities are all welcome!

Who is on The Crusaders' side?

Already signed up are King Richard of England and King Philip of France

Who will they be fighting against?

The Muslims (also known as Saracens) who are led by Saladin, the ruler of Egypt and Syria. He is a tough opponent.

Can you trust us?

Absolutely! This will be our third Crusade to the Holy Land.

First Crusade 1096-1099

A successful trip. The Pope asked The Crusaders to take back the Holy Land from the Muslims. Thousands of Crusaders helped capture the city and set up the Latin Kingdom of Jerusalem.

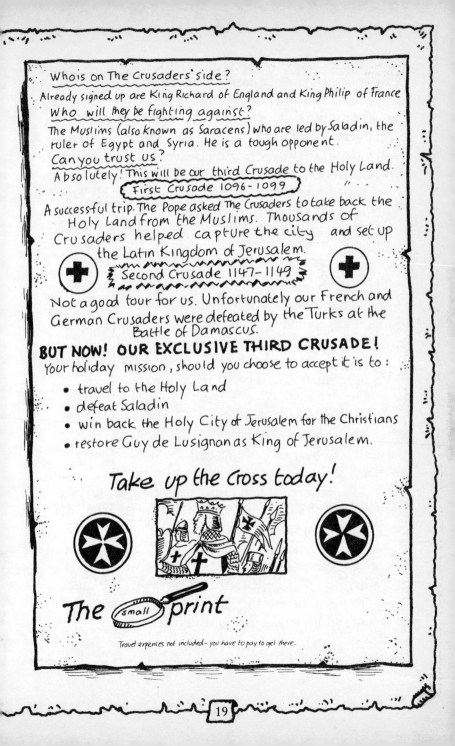

Second Crusade 1147-1149

Not a good tour for us. Unfortunately our French and German Crusaders were defeated by the Turks at the Battle of Damascus.

BUT NOW! OUR EXCLUSIVE THIRD CRUSADE!

Your holiday mission, should you choose to accept it is to:

- travel to the Holy Land
- defeat Saladin
- win back the Holy City of Jerusalem for the Christians
- restore Guy de Lusignan as King of Jerusalem.

Take up the Cross today!

The small print

Travel expenses not included - you have to pay to get there.

Earl David obviously hasn't read the small print. I've told him that this Crusade will cost him a fortune, but he won't listen.

Robert is mad keen to go as well, but I put my foot down about the cost of that. (Unfortunately I put my foot down on Earl David's toe, which didn't do his gout any good.) Earl David agreed with me. He's also worried that the Sheriff of Nottingham has got his eyes on the Huntingdon estates. I can see the Earl's problem:

- The Sheriff is a big buddy of Prince John
- While Big Brother, Richard, is away at the wars, John might get some funny ideas
- If anything happens to Earl David, one of John's funny ideas might be to make the Sheriff, or one of his other mates, Earl of Huntingdon.

Earl David wants Robert to stay at home and look after his estates, so he won't let Robert go on the Crusade. Robert is now in a sulk.

King Richard's been raising money for the Crusade. He's been selling off land, jobs and titles like there's no tomorrow. He's been taxing everyone (me included!) and fining people for not volunteering to go on the Crusade. He's even said that he'll sell London, if he can find a buyer for it!

What a nerve, eh? Richard nips over from France, gets crowned, takes everyone's money and says, "Thanks a lot, ta-ta, cheerio, I'm off!"

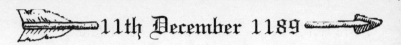

11th December 1189

I had to go to Dover to see Earl David aboard the ship, bound for the Crusade. Cousin Basil is going across to France with Richard first to make all the final preparations. Richard is supposed to be meeting up with King Philip Augustus of France. There'll be fur flying at that meeting. By all accounts, Richard and Philip get on like two cats in a bag.

The whole scene at Dover was organised chaos. There seemed to be scores of ships and thousands of sailors swearing good ripe sea oaths at each other and trying to load hundreds of horses, tons of food and drink, and great piles of weapons. Meanwhile, thousands of soldiers were standing round gawping and getting in the way.

It's obvious that this Crusade is going to cost a pretty fortune. And my taxes have paid for some of it!

Basil waved goodbye and promised to keep in touch.

14th February 1190

I hate these long winter evenings. There's nothing to do except sit round the fire with a few candles and play board games.

Robert loves board games, as long as they're not too complicated. I tried to introduce him to chess (which Crusaders brought back from the Holy Land) but Robert is useless at it – he calls knights "horsies" and can never work out which way they go.

So we went back to Three Men's Morris, where you have nine holes on a board and all you have to do is get three pieces in a row without being blocked*.

Robert's favourite game is queek, where you throw pebbles on to a chess board and bet whether they'll land on a black or white square. He plays this game with Marian. When she loses, she shouts, "Wats!" and "Oh, dwat!" Then she blushes and says, "Oh, pardon my Fwench."

Robin laughs just as much when he loses as when he wins, but there's no skill in a game like this and I get bored out of my skull.

* Exactly as we now play noughts and crosses.

21st June 1190

JOHN COLLARS CASTLE!

In a daring move, Prince John has seized Nottingham Castle from King Richard's men. As Sherwood Forest belongs to John and he already owns several other castles in the area, this puts him in a very powerful position.

Our Political Correspondent says:

The Sheriff of Nottingham and his henchman Sir Guy of Gisborne are probably behind this move. The Sheriff is a friend of Prince John and is taking advantage of King Richard's absence to add to his power base.

The Sheriff hates the Saxons and treats them like dirt. This is because they keep teasing him.

The Saxons called Nottingham "Snottingham", but when the Normans came over and asked the name of the place, some Saxon told them, "It's Snottingham," and they thought he said, "It's Nottingham", so they got the name wrong on all their maps. Of course, Normans never admit they've made a mistake, so they insist on calling it Nottingham – but the Saxons still call it Snottingham, and whenever they see the Sheriff of Snottingham they shout out, "Hey up, Snotty!" and run off laughing.

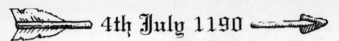

I've just received a chain mail from Cousin Basil.

MICROHARD CHAIN MAIL MESSAGE
From   Basil Count de Money
          (bas@crusade.net)
Date   4 July 1190, 10.10am
To   len.dusomoney@huntingdon.com
Subject: Crusade

We're finally off!
   Richard and Philip Augustus met up at
the Abbey of Vezelay (near Paris). We all
said a few prayers and now we've begun the
trip. We're marching to Marseille to meet
the English fleet. The French are off to
Genoa, and then we'll all meet up at
Messina in Sicily. After that, it's on to
the Holy Land to see if "Salad-is-in" (one
of Richard's jokes - everyone had to laugh
or else).
   Mind you, it's not all good news. I'm
afraid your boss, old Earl David, won't be
coming with us. He hadn't been on a horse
for so long that when he tried to mount up
today, he fell straight off the other side
and broke his neck. You'd better tell that
silly ass Robert to get his armour polished
and come out to join us.
   Yours, as ready as a fox outside a hen-
house,
   Basil

I showed Basil's news to Robert.

"Oh, poor old chap!" he said.

I pointed out that now that his uncle was dead, *he* was the Earl of Huntingdon. (I suppose that makes Marian the Earl's Girl.)

He said, "Oh crikey, I suppose I am. That means I can go on the Crusade. Whoopee!"

I tried to talk Earl Robert out of going with the Crusade. I said that if he turned his back for a minute, the Sheriff would steal his lands and all the peasants would suffer. Earl Robert said he was sorry, but a chap had to do what a chap had to do, don'tcherknow.

"Anyway," Robert went on, "it was my uncle who gave you your bally job, and now he's dead, you're working for me. So if I say I'm going on the Crusade, I'm bally well going on the Crusade. And if you don't stop moaning, I'll find someone else to look after my estates. So there!"

I shut up.

So now my new boss is off somewhere practising sword strokes, shouting things like, "Have at you, Saracen scum", and Marian's locked herself in her room to have a jolly good cry.

What am I doing here?

I'm sitting under a dripping tree. I've got a tree root sticking in my back and a bottom full of pine needles.

I said there'd be trouble from the Sheriff, and I was right. On Earl Robert and Marian's wedding day we were all at church, so of course nobody was carrying any weapons. The priest was droning on in Latin and I was wondering where I'd put the ring when the doors burst open and in came the Sheriff, Guy of Gisborne and a bunch of heavies, all armed to the teeth.

The Sheriff said the Earl of Huntingdon had been made an outlaw for plotting against Prince John, and all his lands and titles had been given to Sir Guy of Gisborne (who was grinning like anything).

I was just about to tell Earl Robert that it was all a put-up job and would never stand up in court when the silly ass lost his temper.

"Oooh, fibs!" he shouted, "rotten beastly fibs! You can tell Prince John that I serve King Richard, and if you make me a bally outlaw, I shall bally well go and hide in the forest and fight you until the King comes back, so there. Marian my love, will you wait for me?"

She was all for it, the romantic fool. "Oh, yes, Wobin. And when King Wichard weturns, he shall mawwy us himself!"

Earl Robert picked up a bench and started swinging it about like a madman. He gave Sir Guy a good hard clout on the ear and knocked the Sheriff into the font. After that things got a bit confused.

So now here we are in Sherwood Forest, worse luck. To begin with, Earl Robert was cheesed off that he couldn't go on the Crusade after all, but then he got cheerier and said chins up and never mind, we would live as free men in the jolly old Greenwood, what! Who would choose to sleep on a feather mattress in an earl's palace, he said, when he could rest on soft leaves under swaying branches beneath the open sky?

What a twit!

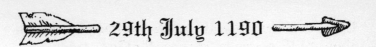

29th July 1190

Earl Robert is full of plans, all of them daft.

"The Sheriff has made me an outlaw," he said this morning, "so I'll jolly well be an outlaw." He thought for a minute. "What is an outlaw, exactly?"

I said an outlaw had to live outside the law. The law wouldn't protect him, and if somebody stole from him or killed him, they wouldn't be punished. In fact, they'd be rewarded. Anyone who killed an outlaw could claim five shillings, the same reward as for killing a wolf. So another name for outlaw was "wolf's head".

I explained that an outlaw's property went to the King, and only the King could grant him a pardon.

"Well, I don't care," said Earl Robert. "I'll live here in Sherwood Forest and lead King Richard's loyal subjects in raids against the Sheriff and that rotter Gisborne."

"They'll know who you are," I told him.

"Then I shall give myself a new outlaw name. I shall call myself Robin, to remind me of Marian. And my second name will remind me that I must always be in disguise." He looked at the clothes he was wearing. "I've got it! I shall call myself... Robin Tights!"

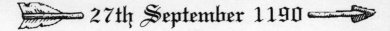

Some of the other outlaws who live here in Sherwood Forest have joined me and Earl Robert... sorry, Robin Hood (ha!). They like him because although he's a Norman toff he doesn't treat them like dirt.

WILL SCARLET

MUCH THE MILLER'S SON

Scarlet is short for "Scathelocke", which means "burnt hair" because Will Scarlet is a redhead. Get it?

Much the Miller's Son is just short.

30th September 1190

Sherwood Forest is a big place. I've been making a map of it. I let Much the Miller's Son do the trees.

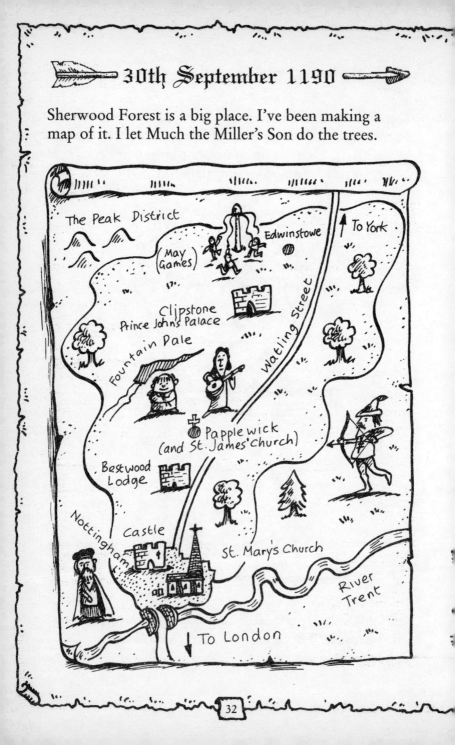

The Peak District

May Games

Edwinstowe

↑ To York

Watling Street

Clipstone
Prince John's Palace

Fountain Dale

✠ Papplewick
(and St. James' Church)

Bestwood Lodge

Nottingham Castle

St. Mary's Church

River Trent

↓ To London

It isn't all woodland – there are open spaces as well, but it is very wild. There are hundreds of places to hide, and travellers don't like going through it because there are a lot of outlaws living in Sherwood Forest. This isn't really surprising when you think how strict the Forest Laws are.

Most of the Royal Forests belong to King Richard, but Sherwood belongs to Prince John. Nobody except John (and his friends) is allowed to hunt in Sherwood. On the other hand, John isn't allowed to hunt anywhere else. That's why he likes to make sure nobody else goes hunting in his forest, so there are lots of laws to put people off poaching. For instance:

CRIME : PUNISHMENTE

Killing a boar or a stag → Having ye eyes putte oute

Takeing a hare → A fine of twenty shillinges

Takeing a rabbit → A fine of ten shillinges

Using a bowe and arrows in ye foreste → Having a fingere and thumb cut offe

Living in the forest hasn't been too bad so far. Most of the outlaws who've joined us are pretty handy with a bow. Robin has turned out to be a crack shot (I knew he must be good at something – I suppose when he was a rich idle layabout, he had a lot of time to practice archery). Any time we're hungry, someone just goes out and shoots a deer. I'm getting pretty fed up with having nothing to eat but venison.

Now winter's coming, it's getting harder to find nuts and berries. We need money to buy things, but all Robin's wealth from the Huntingdon estates has been confiscated by the Sheriff.

I suggested that we should make some money by charging people to cross the bridge over the stream near our camp. It's really just an old tree that somebody chopped down so that it fell across the stream. So I made a sign. Then Robin stood at one end of the bridge to wait for a traveller to pass by, and the rest of the outlaws went and hid in the bushes, giggling.

Just as we were getting fed up, a huge bloke turned up and started to cross the bridge.

All the outlaws came charging out of the bushes with arrows at the ready, but Robin ordered them to put their bows away. He asked the big bloke to join us. The big bloke then said he couldn't join us, he'd come to join Robin Hood.

Robin declared, "But *I'm* Robin Hood."

The big bloke looked him up and down. "Give over," he scoffed.

Robin protested, "No, I am, really."

Then the big bloke said his name was John Little.

Of course, Will Scarlet and the lads nearly wet themselves laughing. "Then we shall call you Little John," cried Will, "because you're so big!"

Such wit!

Little John said he'd become an outlaw when he caught Guy of Gisborne whipping one of his peasants, and punched his lights out. So all the outlaws sang "For he's a jolly good fellow" and welcomed him to the gang.

I have to admit, Robin has a gift for dealing with people. He got made to look a right charlie today, but he was so good-natured about it, he actually got more respect from the lads than if he'd won.

```
MICROHARD CHAIN MAIL MESSAGE
From      Basil Count de Money
          (bas@crusade.net)
Date      26 March 1191, 3.15pm
To        len.dusomoney@sherwood.com
Subject   Arguments!
```

Here we are in Sicily. When we arrived,
the locals locked up some of the lads and
overcharged us for food, so Richard
decided to conquer them. Then Richard and
King Philip had a bust-up. The word is
that Richard is going to marry someone
called Berengaria (what a strange name).
She's the daughter of King Sancho the
Strong of Navarre (another strange name).
The problem is that Richard is already
engaged to Philip's sister, Alice. In fact
he's been engaged to her for over twenty
years!

He's been finding excuses not to marry
her:

1) he's got to wash his hair

2) his mum won't let him out

3) Alice used to be his dad's
girlfriend.

Philip has finally realised that Richard
is serious about not marrying Alice, so
he's having a big sulk. On this happy
note, we're off to the Holy Land!

Yours, as keen as a flea in a doublet,

Basil

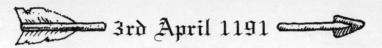

3rd April 1191

Little John brought a traveller back to camp today. He turned out to be a public relations consultant. He told Robin that we had an image problem.

"People have a negative view of outlaws," he told Robin. "They associate them with hostility and being robbed."

"Shut up and give us your money before I thump you," said Little John.

"See what I mean?" said the PR man.

He then tried to get Robin to dress all the outlaws in yellow. "It's such a soothing colour," he said.

I pointed out that it would be a bit difficult for outlaws dressed like bananas to hide in the forest. The PR type had to admit I had a point.

In the end he and Robin settled on Lincoln Green, which would be hard to spot among the trees (though Will Scarlet went all sulky because green just *didn't go* with his red hair).

Mind you, I still think it was a mistake to let the PR chappie give the lads a makeover.

11th April 1191

The Sheriff of Nottingham and some of his pals are no better than upper-class gangsters! With King Richard out of the way, they think they can can break the law whenever they like and get away with it! Two of their favourite scams are:

EXTORTION

Give me some money or I'll beat you up.

PROTECTION RACKET

Give me some money and I'll make sure nobody beats you up. —especially me!

Anybody who tries to stop them is either bribed, threatened or killed. So Robin has decided that from now on, we're going to rob from the rich and give to the poor.

I couldn't believe my ears. When he said "give to the poor", surely he meant "lend to the poor at a crippling rate of interest"?

Robin said no. He said he felt guilty about:

a) being a Norman (and therefore a toff)

b) not going on the Crusade.

He was going to take money from the Normans (who had too much of it) and give it to the Saxons (who didn't have enough).

The whole thing sounded perfectly potty to me. Was this supposed to be some sort of tax dodge? Outlaws were meant to rob people! I said I was right alongside the idea of robbing the rich, it was good sound financial policy – but what was wrong with robbing the poor as well? Admittedly, they didn't have as much money, but there were more of them…

Robin got very high and mighty and said that he was fighting the good fight for Good Old King Richard, what! and it was his duty to fight injustice, right wrongs and succour the needy.

I told Robin that if he gives money to the needy, he'll be the sucker.

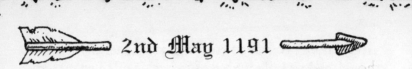

2nd May 1191

Robin's decided we can all go on an outlaws' outing, so here we are in Edwinstowe for the May Games.

We arrived just in time to see the girls of the village dancing round the Maypole. After that there was more dancing, but most of the lads joined in with the sports instead.

I had a go at stoolball, and hit one of the girls. She said I could have a cake or a kiss. She had a face like a horse, so I said I'd have the cake.

Then some peasants did a Morris dance, leaping about and waving hankies in the air. I don't know who Morris is, but if I was his mother, I'd be worried.

Then the Mummers' plays started. I've always thought these are pretty childish, but Robin was like a dog with two tails. He booed when the Saracen killed St George (the baddie used to be the Devil, but since the Crusades started it's been a Saracen). He shouted "I do believe in fairies" when the doctor brought St George back to life again. He cheered when St George killed the Saracen. Then he cried like a baby when I told him the play had finished and it was time to go home.

```
MICROHARD CHAIN MAIL MESSAGE
From      Basil Count de Money
          (bas@crusade.net)
Date      26 May 1191, 6.15pm
To        len.dusomoney@sherwood.com
Subject   Trouble!
```

Our journey across the Mediterranean Sea was not good. Half our ships (including Berengaria's) got blown across to Cyprus in a storm. When Richard turned up and asked for his fiancée back, the Emperor of Cyprus (who's called Isaac Comnenus – *another* silly name) attacked us! His soldiers didn't stand a chance and Isaac scarpered. Then Richard married Berengaria and she was crowned Queen of England.

The honeymoon was more like a stag night. Richard decided to conquer Cyprus and we had fifteen days of fighting and pillaging! Ex-Emperor Isaac surrendered on condition that Richard wouldn't put him in iron chains. Richard agreed – he had silver chains made and put Isaac in those instead. What a sense of humour!

Now we're finally off to the Holy Land. About time!

Yours, as fresh as a ferret at a rabbit hole,

Basil

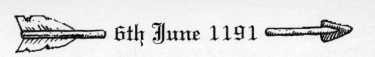

We've got a new outlaw in the band, for all the use he is. It happened this way.

Robin and I were down in the forest stopping travellers and asking them for tolls as per usual, when this lad came drooping along. He was sobbing like a sheep with wind, and he kept shouting, "Oh, woe is me" and "Lackaday" and similar.

Robin stopped him and said, "Does something ail thee, my friend?" (What a mind, eh? Sharp as a razor.)

The drippy article unstrapped a lute* from his back and sang:

> "I love a maiden truly
> And 'tis for her I pine,
> For a rich old toff
> Has carried her off,
> The filthy Norman swine."

Oh dear, I thought, that's all we need – not just a poophead, but a poet as well.

*A stringed instrument, a sort of medieval guitar.

The miserable object told us he was a wandering minstrel and his name was Alan A'Dale. Then he sang:

We swore that we'd never be parted,
But he stole her, the dirty old rat,
She's as fresh as a rose
With a lovely pink nose
While he's ninety-seven and fat.

Robin said "Chin up, old fellow," and told him about Marian and how he hadn't seen her in AGES and then he started blubbering as well.

This big drip of a minstrel then asked if we could rescue his girlfriend. I asked what was it worth. He said he had no money, but he would swear to be Robin's servant. Big deal, I thought, but Robin was all for it. I must have a word with him about harsh economic realities.

MICROHARD CHAIN MAIL MESSAGE
From   Basil Count de Money
          (bas@crusade.net)
Date   8 June 1191, 10.05am
To   len.dusomoney@sherwood.com
Subject   Siege of Acre

We've finally arrived in the Holy Land!
We've landed outside the port of Acre.
The city has been under siege by the
Christians for eighteen months.

Acre is very impressive. It has massive
walls and lots of towers. No wonder the
Muslim defenders have been able to hold
out for so long.

But now Richard's here. The Muslims have
heard about him and are VERY worried. They
should be!

Yours, up for some serious Saracen-
bashing,
   Basil

P.S. I've downloaded a map so you can
follow our progress!

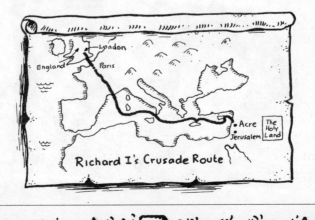

Richard I's Crusade Route

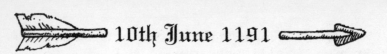

After breakfast this morning (venison sausages), Robin blew his horn and off we went to Papplewick church to rescue Alan A'Dale's sweetheart.

When we all piled in with bows drawn, the bridgegroom-to-be scarpered through the vestry. The Bishop said he couldn't marry the girl to Alan A'Dale because the marriage banns hadn't been read out three times. So Robin gave the Bishop's frock and hat to Little John, who read the banns out seven times just to be on the safe side while the congregation laughed themselves into fits (they don't get out much in Papplewick). Robin gave the bride away and Little John married her to Alan A'Dale and everyone cheered like mad.

After the service some toothless old crone came up cackling, "God bless ee, maister, Oi haven't laughed so much in all my days. Oi do think thee should be called Robin Hood and his Merry Men."

Robin thought this was very funny, and said that's what we would call ourselves from now on.

If you ask me, it makes us sound like a bunch of third-rate clowns.

```
MICROHARD CHAIN MAIL MESSAGE
From      Basil Count de Money
          (bas@crusade.net)
Date      12 July 1191, 10.33pm
To        len.dusomoney@sherwood.com
Subject   VICTORY!
```

Acre is ours - not before time!

All my hair and fingernails fell out during the siege! I had a fever called "arnaldia". Richard and King Philip also caught it. We ended up looking like right slapheads. I couldn't even pick my nose properly!

The Muslim commanders in Acre finally realised that they couldn't hold out any longer against our siege engines. Saladin and his army couldn't do anything to help them either, so they surrendered.

The Muslims have now got to pay 200,000 gold pieces as part of the surrender agreement. Until the money is paid, the three thousand Muslims in the city will be kept hostage.

Saladin is not happy with these terms, but tough luck - he's lost!

Yours, as bald as a baby's botty but as happy as a big yeehah,

Basil

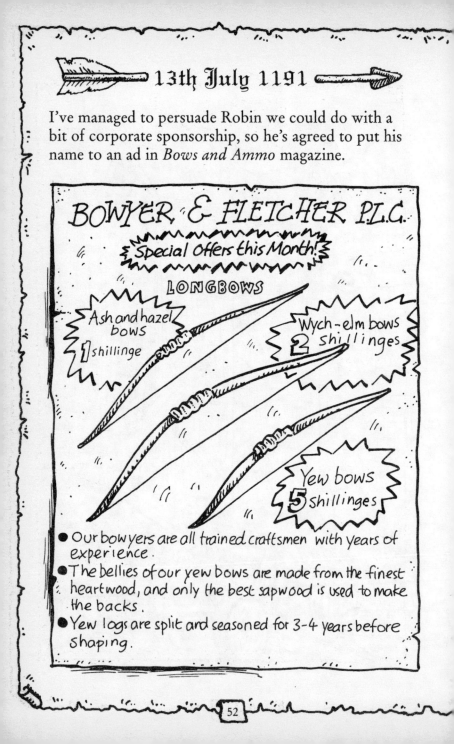

13th July 1191

I've managed to persuade Robin we could do with a bit of corporate sponsorship, so he's agreed to put his name to an ad in *Bows and Ammo* magazine.

BOWYER & FLETCHER P.L.C.

Special Offers this Month!

LONGBOWS

Ash and hazel bows
1 shillinge

Wych-elm bows
2 shillinges

Yew bows
5 shillinges

- Our bowyers are all trained craftsmen with years of experience.
- The bellies of our yew bows are made from the finest heartwood, and only the best sapwood is used to make the backs.
- Yew logs are split and seasoned for 3-4 years before shaping.

BOWSTRINGS

All our bowstrings are made from best quality hemp and flax, impregnated with beeswax.

ARROWS

- Make your own choice from our range of ash, alder or poplar arrows.
- All our glue is made from bluebell bulbs. Accept no substitutes!
- Arrows fletched with crow feathers 1 shillinge per dozen.
- Arrows fletched with swan or peacock feathers 2 shillinges per dozen.
- Our top-of-the-range arrows with goose-feather flights now available at only 4 shillinges per dozen!

Robin Hood says, "Why settle for anything less?"

```
MICROHARD CHAIN MAIL MESSAGE
From      Basil Count de Money
          (bas@crusade.net)
Date      3 August 1191, 10.27pm
To        len.dusomoney@sherwood.com
Subject   Arguments!
```

A while ago, Richard spotted that Leopold of
Austria was flying his flag from one of the
city's towers. Richard got all jealous and said
it was *his* brilliant leadership that won the
siege of Acre and no one except him could put
their flag up, so there – especially Leopold
who's not even a King, only a Duke.

Leopold said he was jolly well going to fly
his flag. Richard said he'd tear Leopold's flag
down. Then the following top level diplomatic
discussions took place.

LEOPOLD: Right, go on then. I dare you.
RICHARD: Right then, I will.
LEOPOLD: Go on then.
RICHARD: I will then!

So Richard tore down Leopold's flag and threw
it in the moat. Leo burst into tears and said
he knew when he wasn't wanted, packed his bags
and headed home. Oh dear, I thought – his
Kingship's temper will get him (and us) into
big trouble one of these days.

Then King Philip announced that he was fed up
and was going back to France. So he's packed
his bags and gone home too, taking loads of his
men. It's going to be a difficult job to defeat
Saladin now.

Yours, as confused as a fish in a thorn bush,
Basil

P.S. Saladin STILL hasn't paid up! Richard is
getting very annoyed and you know what his
temper is like!

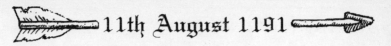

Robin's a law-abiding soul at heart. He robbed a tax collector today, which reminded him he hadn't filled in his tax forms from last year.

I pointed out that as his accountant, it was my job to make sure he didn't pay taxes – or at any rate, paid as little as possible. What's more, by not paying taxes he was doing the Sheriff a favour because we'd only nick the money back anyway.

In the end I had to write it down for him.

IF WE PAY TAXES:
STEP 1) We give the money to the Sheriff
STEP 2) He has to think up a plan to keep the money safe from us
STEP 3) We have to think up a plan to pinch the money – that's a lot of man-hours
STEP 4) He sends the taxes to Prince John
STEP 5) We ambush the soldiers guarding the taxes
STEP 6) We use up lots of arrows (which we'd put down as expenses anyway)
STEP 7) Some of the soldiers get killed.

BUT, if we didn't pay taxes in the first place, the Sheriff wouldn't have to make up a plan, we wouldn't have to spend money on arrows, the Sheriff's soldiers wouldn't get killed and we'd still have the money!

Isn't accountancy wonderful!

```
MICROHARD CHAIN MAIL MESSAGE
From      Basil Count de Money
          (bas@crusade.net)
Date      20 August 1191, 7.45pm
To        len.dusomoney@sherwood.com
Subject   Slaughter at Acre
```

Saladin was supposed to pay up for the prisoners by this morning. But he didn't.

Richard was furious. We need to set off for Jerusalem – we've spent far too long here. So what could we do with three thousand Muslims? We couldn't leave them here or take them with us. And if we released them, they'd only return and fight us.

Richard came up with a solution. At midday, we roped the prisoners (men, women and children) together and marched them out of the city. Then we killed them. All three thousand.

Saladin now knows that Richard isn't someone to be messed with.

Yours, a bit shocked,

Basil

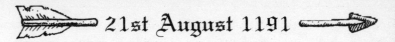

21st August 1191

Robin still won't hear a word against King Richard, but reading Basil's chain mail really upset him. He called an outlaws' meeting last night and said that we shouldn't hurt anybody just to make them give us all their money.

I said, fair enough, but if people refused to give us their money, then it was all right to hurt them, wasn't it?

Robin had to think about that for a bit. Eventually he said "Yes," but he didn't look too happy.

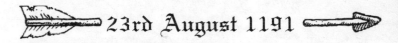

23rd August 1191

Little John went out this morning for a bit of robbery-with-not-too-much-violence. When he came back, he had a sorry-looking specimen in tow.

The stranger was a knight. At least, he was wearing armour and riding a horse, but the armour had holes in it and the horse looked as if it was about two canters and a trot away from being catfood.

The poor knight said his name was Sir Richard of the Lee. His son had accidentally killed another knight at a tournament, and Sir Richard had to pay a fine of four hundred quid which he'd borrowed from St Mary's Abbey at York.

I said he must have been barmy to borrow from the Church. Abbots are loan sharks, and anybody who doesn't pay back a loan on time is liable to find himself surrounded by burly monks with clubs and given a right good blessing.

Robin said, "Never mind, old fellow. I'll lend you four hundred pounds."

I tried to talk some sense into Robin. He didn't know this knight from Adam – was it wise to risk an unsecured loan? And what about the interest repayments…?

Sir Richard said Robin was a noble fellow and he'd repay him when he could. So Robin sent him off to York to pay the Abbot and told him to call in on his way back to tell us how he'd got on.

```
MICROHARD CHAIN MAIL MESSAGE
From      Basil Count de Money
          (bas@crusade.net)
Date      7 September 1191, 9.47pm
To        len.dusomoney@sherwood.com
Subject   Battle of Arsuf
```

We are the champions!

We've spent the past few days marching towards Jaffa. We'd reached Arsuf when Saladin attacked us. He had thirty thousand soldiers against our fifteen thousand. However, numbers didn't matter. Richard took control of the battle and we hammered Saladin's army! We killed over seven thousand of them.

We're not going on to Jerusalem yet. We need a base so we're going to Jaffa. The Holy Land is going to be ours and Saladin isn't singing any more!

Yours, as chuffed as a boar in a barley field,

Basil

We were expecting Sir Richard back today, but instead Little John brought back a couple of fat monks from St Mary's Abbey at York. Robin insisted they had dinner with us (venison, just for a change).

After dinner Robin asked them to pay for their meal, and they said things like "Golly, is that the time" and "Must dash". Then Little John strung his bow in a meaningful sort of way. The monks suddenly started whining that they were poor and their saddlebags were empty. So Will Scarlet had a shufty and found they were carrying eight hundred quid.

"Heavens," said the monks unconvincingly, "how did that get there? It's a miracle!"

I said that if these monks were from St Mary's Abbey, they must have brought Sir Richard's repayment to save him the trouble. The monks started to protest, so we sent them on their way with a flea in the ear and a few arrows up the bum.

When Sir Richard turned up, Robin told him not to worry about repaying the loan and gave him another four hundred pounds to buy himself a decent horse.

So we bring this bloke in to rob him and end up giving him eight hundred smackers. I give up!

Boxing Day 1191

Sir Richard was so grateful to Robin that he invited us all back to his castle for Christmas. His castle's a bit draughty, but it beats sleeping under a bush.

On Christmas Eve Marian turned up. She and Robin went off somewhere with a sprig of mistletoe and there was a lot of giggling.

This morning, we all trooped off to church and Sir Richard broke open the alms box in the church and gave all the money to the poor. Then we went out skating.

Will Scarlet made the skates out of cattle bones. I could hardly stand up on mine so I just pushed myself along with a stick, but Will Scarlet strapped his skates to his feet and went racing about like nobody's business. Some of the others used their poles as lances and started having ice-jousts on piggyback while Much the Miller's Son threw snowballs at them.

Outlaws? They're just a bunch of big kids.

Easter Day 1192

We're in York for a few days. Robin wanted to watch the Miracle Plays.

This is a sort of church panto. All the priests dress up as Noah and King Herod etc and act out Bible stories in the church (or in the churchyard if the weather's nice). The Bible is written in Latin and most people don't understand it, so the plays help people grasp the stories about Jesus and so on. I can't be doing with all this happy-clappy stuff myself.

The other outlaws went off to find some sport. There's usually a game of campball going at Easter. You can have hundreds of people on a side, all chasing a leather ball the size of a clenched fist. You can throw the ball, but not kick it. When a player gets the ball he sets off for his opponent's goal while everybody else tries to kill him (or each other). Since the goals can be miles apart, games usually last all day. Scores are usually low, but casualties are high.

11th April 1192

With King Richard out of the way, the Sheriff of Nottingham and his cronies think they can do just what they like!

These so-called knights are supposed to behave honourably, and live by a strict set of rules:

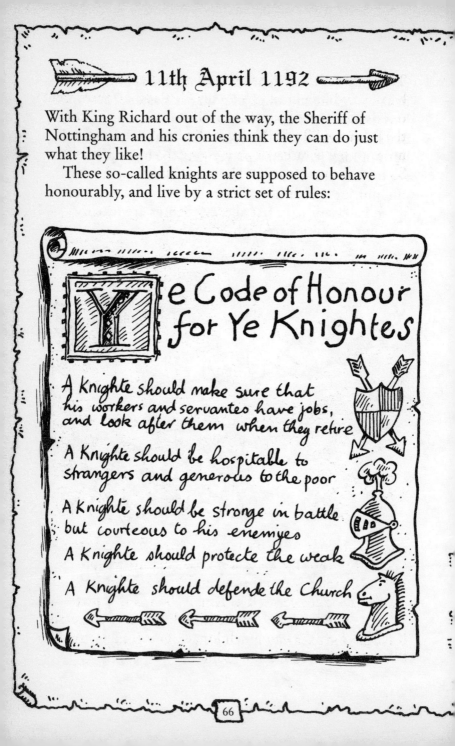

Ye Code of Honour for Ye Knightes

A Knighte should make sure that his workers and servantes have jobs, and look after them when they retire

A Knighte should be hospitable to strangers and generous to the poor

A Knighte should be stronge in battle but courteous to his enemyes

A Knighte should protecte the weak

A Knighte should defende the Church

The trouble is that when King Richard called on the barons and knights to go on his Crusade, all the decent ones said, "Oh, all right then, if you insist," and off they went, while all the cowardly layabouts sent in notes to say they'd got a verucca and stayed behind. So now the cowardly layabouts are in charge!

I sent a chain mail to Basil today. I told him that the Sheriff of Nottingham is still throwing his weight about (there's a lot to throw) and Prince John is starting to fancy himself as King. The word is that John is getting support from King Philip of France, so if Richard stays away much longer, he's going to find he's a King without a kingdom.

MICROHARD CHAIN MAIL MESSAGE
From   Basil Count de Money
          (bas@crusade.net)
Date   20 April 1192, 7.36pm
To   len.dusomoney@sherwood.com
Subject   Not a very Happy Easter

I told Richard your news about John. He
wasn't happy. He gathered all his
commanders together for a high-level
meeting at Ascalon. He told them that he
was going to go home.

The other Crusaders said he was a party-
pooper etc, and offered the throne to
Conrad of Montferrat. Conrad said, "Yes, oh
yes, oh yes!" I think he was quite pleased.

So, with the King thing sorted out, it
looks as though we're coming home!

Yours, as cheered up as a goose at a
vegetarian banquet,
Basil

MICROHARD CHAIN MAIL MESSAGE
From   Basil Count de Money
          (bas@crusade.net)
Date   28 April 1192, 7.45pm
To   len.dusomoney@sherwood.com
Subject   Bad news

Cancel the coming home bit.

Conrad is dead. He's been killed by two
assassins. There's no one to lead the
Crusade except Richard. So we've got to
stay.

Yours, as cross as a Crusader's coat,
Basil

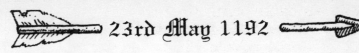

Alan A'Dale insisted on singing me his new song today. It goes:

"With a hey nonny no
And a nonny nonny no,
With a hey no nonny no hey...
And a nonny nonny no
Hey hey nonny no
And a nonny nonny no no nay... All together now!...
With a hey nonny no
And a nonny nonny no,
With a hey no nonny no hey...
And a nonny nonny no
Hey hey nonny no
And a nonny nonny no no,
Hey!"

He said, did I think that was good, hey?
    I said, "Nonny nonny NO!!!!"

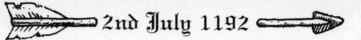

2nd July 1192

How Robin Hood Met Friar Tuck
A Ballad By Alan A'Dale

I'll tell you a tale of Bold Robin,
An outlaw, as some folks would say,
He was strong as an ox,
He wore Lincoln green socks,
And he lived over Snottingham way.

One day he was pulling his longbow
(It was long as a longbow could be),
When Will Scarlet said, "Hood!
There's a Friar in the wood!"
And Robin said, "This, I must see!"

They found the fat Friar by the river
Singing hymns fit to waken the dead,
He was round, he was tanned,
He'd a sword in his hand
And a helmet on top of his head.

"What do they call you?" asked Robin,
The Friar said, "I'll give you a clue,
Friar Tuck is my name,
And fighting's my game
And anyway, what's it to you?"

"Do me a favour," said Robin,
"And carry me over this flood,
You can take me across
Like a knight on his hoss
'Cos a Friar is supposed to do good."

The friar made a back for bold Robin
And carried him over the beck*,
But upon reaching land
Robin felt a strong hand
At his throat, and a sword at his neck.

The Friar said, "Now then, young master,
I've carried you over one way,
Now you'll carry me back
Or I swear I will hack
You to bits. No offence, as they say."

Robin struggled to lift the fat Friar,
He must have weighed nearly a ton,
His strength soon diminished –
Before he had finished,
He wished that he'd never begun.

Then Robin got back on the Friar
And roared, "Take me back over there!"
But quick as a wink,
He was dropped in the drink –
"You can sink!" said Tuck. "See if I care!"

Robin Hood blew his horn in a twinkling,
And his outlaws ran up by the score,
And when they saw Robin
In that stream a'bobbin
They laughed 'til their insides were sore.

* Northern dialect word for a stream, or brook.

Robin cried, "Join my band, worthy Friar!
You're a fighter, as well as a priest,
And I have need of both,
So swear me an oath,
And come join us all in a feast!"

The Friar agreed to this bargain,
And he knelt down at Robin Hood's feet,
"I'm your man without fail
While you still have good ale,
And venison for me to eat!"

That creep Alan A'Dale has been writing in my diary!
I was going to write about Robin meeting Friar Tuck,
and he's spoilt it! I'll pay him back, just you wait!

```
MICROHARD CHAIN MAIL MESSAGE
From      Basil Count de Money
          (bas@crusade.net)
Date      9 August 1192, 7.54pm
To        len.dusomoney@sherwood.com
Subject   A lot to tell you
```

Sorry I've not been in touch. The chain
mail link has been down. There's lots to
tell you:
   1) Saladin put the squeeze on Jaffa and
   captured it
   2) Richard captured it back
   3) Saladin and Richard fell ill
   4) Best of all, they've signed a three-
   year truce.
   We keep the coastal cities and the
Muslims keep Jerusalem, but Christian
pilgrims can still visit the city.
Richard's not going to go to Jerusalem. He
said if he couldn't capture it, he didn't
want to see it.
   It seems to me that there's been a lot
of death in exchange for not a lot else.
   Yours, as tired as a tickled trout,
   Basil

I've been talking to Friar Tuck. I asked him, what was a priest doing in an outlaw band? He asked me, what was an accountant doing in an outlaw band? I said fair enough.

Friar Tuck said in any case, he'd be better off than the rest of us if we got caught. Robin and I and all the others would be sent to trial in the criminal courts, but a friar can only be tried in the Church courts, and the worst they could do would be to defrock him. I said what, pull his cassock off? He said no, it meant they could stop him being a priest anymore.

I asked him which abbey he was from. He said friars didn't live in abbeys, they were wandering priests. Monks lived in abbeys. There were basically two sorts of monks – your Cistercians and your Benedictines. Your Benedictines (who follow the teachings of St Benedict) were filthy rich. Your Cistercians said men of God shouldn't be rolling in money and going out partying until 3am etc, so they went and founded their own abbeys where they could sleep on stone mattresses and eat thistles to their hearts' content.

If I ever get a religious calling, I know which lot I'll join!

```
MICROHARD CHAIN MAIL MESSAGE
From     Basil Count de Money
         (bas@crusade.net)
Date     9 October 1192, 8.33am
To       len.dusomoney@sherwood.com
Subject  We're coming home, we're coming
         home!
```

Make sure the goose is getting fat! We should be home in time for Christmas!

We set sail from Acre today (Queen Berengaria left ten days ago).

I'm happy to be getting away from the place, but Richard seems depressed. As we sailed away, he stared back at the Holy Land, sighed and promised he would return. I must say, rather him than me.

Yours, as pleased as a rat in a bucket of bacon rind,

Basil

It turns out that Friar Tuck knows a lot about herbs.
This will be useful if anyone gets sick or wounded*.
He showed me his herb-book.

— FRYAR TUCKE'S LITTEL BOOKE OF HERBES —

ANGELICA
chew ye leaves to relieve ye flatulence

IRIS
• ye rootes are used for makeing ye ink
• ye juice of ye flowers will remoue ye zits
(or ye can dye cloth with itte)

PENNYROYAL
gets ridde of ye fleas

PEONY
drinke ye seeds in wine or ale to stop
bad dreames

PRIMROSE
chew on ye leaves for relief from paine

RUE
cleans oute ye insides

WORMWOOD
• excellente for riddinge ye body of wormes
• as an antidote to poison,
• cures constipation and
stomach ache.

Remind me not to get ill!

* *Doctors were rare and expensive in Robin Hood's day. Poor people
would use herbs as medicine if they got sick.*

27th November 1192

The Ballad of Robin Hood and the Potter
by Alan A'Dale

A potter drove to market on a frosty Autumn day,
To sell his goods in Nottingham he went upon his way,
But deep in Sherwood Forest, on the brakes he had to stand
For an outlaw stood before him with a longbow in hish and.

He said, "My name is Robin Hood. All travellers must pay
A toll to use the forest roads before they pass this way."
The potter said, "I've used this road for twenty years and nine
So you can take your toll and stick it where the sun don't shine!"

They fought upon the muddy road, they fought among the trees,
They fought and fought until they brought each other to their knees,
Then Robin cried, "Hang on a tick! Let's settle for a draw,
I've never met a potter with a punch like yours before."

With that, bold Robin blew his horn — the woods rang with the sound,
'Til all his men came running in from miles and miles around,
And Robin said, "Sir Potter, you have matched me blow for blow!
So let's be friends, and come and have a drink before you go."

The potter said he'd pots to sell in Nottingham that day,
Besides, he'd miss the contest if he lingered on the way,
For all the bowmen in the shire were called on to appear
To win the Silver Arrow as the Archer of the Year.
"By George," cried Robin, "I should like to go and see that sport,
But if I go in Lincoln green, I'll certainly be caught,
That contest I will enter as a potter, in disguise —
I'll win that Silver Arrow right before the Sheriff's eyes!"

They made a bargain — Robin took the potter's pots to sell,
He borrowed...

They made a bargain - Robin took the Potter's pots to sell

I don't believe it! I caught Alan A'Dale writing in my diary AGAIN! If he wants to write his stupid poetry, why doesn't he buy his own diary?

If you want to know what happened when Robin went to Nottingham disguised as the Potter, I'll tell you. He set up a stall in the market. Having the business sense of a duck, he started selling pots for about half what all the other traders were asking. He sold his last five pots to the Sheriff's wife, and she was so chuffed she asked him back to the castle for a cuppa.

He ended up drinking ale with the Sheriff, and asked if he could shoot in the archery contest. The Sheriff roared with laughter at the idea of a potter shooting against his best men, and even lent Robin a bow.

The Sheriff's best archer, Gilbert of the White Hand, stepped up to shoot:

Then the "potter" stepped up:

The Sheriff was a sick as mud. He'd only set the contest up to lure Robin Hood into his clutches. Robin Hood hadn't turned up and now the Sheriff had to give his famous Silver Arrow away to a mere potter! He demanded to know who had taught a potter to shoot like that.

With a straight face, Robin said, "Robin Hood taught me." He offered to take the Sheriff to meet Robin Hood to prove he was telling the truth.

So next day, the Sheriff and his men-at-arms followed the potter into the wood – and right into an ambush.

The lads took all the soldiers' weapons and armour and made them walk back to town in their undies. They took the Sheriff back to our camp and took it in turns to shoot apples off his head for a laugh, and then Robin made him promise to leave us alone (I'll believe that when I see it!) and let him go.

Well, I'm glad Robin's been enjoying himself, but how am I supposed to put that Silver Arrow down in Robin's expenses? Is it income, capital gains or gratuities? Some people are so wrapped up in their own little world they never think about anybody else!

```
MICROHARD CHAIN MAIL MESSAGE
From      Basil Count de Money
          (bas@crusade.net)
Date      5 December 1192, 8.16am
To        len.dusomoney@sherwood.com
Subject Lost - one King!
```

Put the goose on hold! We're not going to
be home for Christmas. Our trip home has
gone seriously pear-shaped.

Richard didn't want to sail all the way
back to England (he gets sea sick) so he
sent the English fleet home. The rest of
us then disguised ourselves as travelling
pilgrims and set off across Europe. This
meant we had to pass through territory
that belongs to Richard's enemies (and
he's got a lot of those).

When we arrived in Austria, we decided
to lay low in Vienna for a bit - but as
soon as I turned my back for two minutes,
Richard disappeared!

Of course, the ruler of Austria is Duke
Leopold, whose banner Richard threw in the
moat at Acre. You don't need a calculator
to work out that Leo's probably getting
his own back!

I suppose I'd better try and find where
Richard's gone.

Yours, as worried as a pig in a pie shop,
Basil

30th December 1192

A message arrived at camp today by carrier pigeon. It went, "Coo, coo… coo-coo… coo."

It was one of Marian's pigeons, the ones that Robin gave her in case she needed to get in touch with him quickly. She thinks that if she says to it, "Tell Wobin to come wight away!" and sends it off, Robin will get the message.

I've tried to explain to her that she needs to *write* the message and *tie* it to the pigeon's *leg*. Still, if she sent a pigeon at all, she must want something. Robin and most of the lads were out looking for rich travellers to nobble, so I strolled over to her dad's manor to find out.

I had to sneak past a couple of men-at-arms lounging by the gate. I crept up to the minstrels' gallery above the main hall. Down below me, I could see Sir Guy of Gisborne. He was wearing several bottles of hair-oil, holding a king-sized bunch of mistletoe and trying to get a kiss from Marian, who was having none of it.

"Unhand me, you wetch!" she snapped. "Wotter! Wuffian! Wogue! Wascal!"

Gisborne said he was going to marry her.

I will never Mawwy you! I would wather dwown myself in the wiver!

Gisborne gave an oily chuckle and said he liked a wench with spirit.

"Wench?" cried Marion. "Who are you calling a spanner?"

Then Gisborne buzzed off to arrange the wedding reception, but he left his men on guard.

As soon as he'd gone, I slipped out of hiding. Marian was positively dancing with rage. I told her I'd come to take her to Robin, but she'd better disguise herself as a page.

"Oh, wight ho!" she cried, clapping her hands in girlish glee. "I can make myself a paper wobe, and wite words all over it…"

"Not a page from a book!" I told her, exasperated. "A page-boy!"

So Marian got dressed up as a page-boy, and as soon as it got dark, we nipped over the back wall of the manor and legged it. Marian shouted, "Yoicks! Tally ho!" and went sprinting off through the woods while I tried to keep up, tripping over brambles and falling in streams. By the time we got back to camp, she was as fresh as a daisy and I was completely wiped out.

To be fair, she gave me full credit. "Len wescued me," she told Robin. "He was so bwave!", which was stretching the truth a little. If that's outlawing, you can keep it. Robin can rescue his own girls in future. I'm off to find some nice money to count.

```
MICROHARD CHAIN MAIL MESSAGE
From      Basil Count de Money
          (bas@crusade.net)
Date      20 February 1193, 8.22am
To        len.dusomoney@sherwood.com
Subject   I've found the King!
```

Well, it took some time, but I've found the King!

King Richard's favourite minstrel, Blondel, had a bright idea. He reckoned there was a song that only he and Richard knew. If he and I went around singing the first verse of the song and we heard anyone singing the second verse, that would be Richard. So for the past few weeks, Blondel and I have been visiting the castles of Germany singing "Fa la la" more times than I want to remember.

Amazingly enough, after weeks of singing our throats out, we finally found Richard! (Thank goodness! If I have to sing that song again I'll go completely nonny no!) It *was* Leo of Austria that locked him up, but Richard reckons that he's going to be handed over to the German Emperor Henry VI any day.

Let everyone know the King is safe!
Yours, with a voice like a squeaky door,
Basil

28th February 1193

A KING'S RANSOM

The government has just received the following ransom note from the German Emperor, Henry VI.

PAY ME 100,000 MARKS OR ELSE the KING gets it

<u>New taxes</u>
In order to raise the 100,000 marks*, the government has announced new taxes:

- Every freeman in England has to pay a quarter of their income
- All churches have to donate their altar plate to be melted down
- Cistercian monks have to donate a whole year's wool crop
- All clergy have to give a tenth of their income.

<u>Do we want our King back?</u>
Ring our readers' survey hotline:
"Yea" ring Freephone 100 000
"No nonny no" ring 0800 0000 (All 0800 calls are charges at £100 per second. This will go towards the ransom. Thank you!)

<u>Other news</u>
Saladin dead – see page 6

* In today's money, this works out at about a HUNDRED BILLION pounds!

10th July 1193

The ransom taxes are squeezing everyone dry!

Robin's doing his best to collect the ransom – he's even been checking his tax returns to make sure I'm not fiddling them (as if I would!) and then sending double what he actually owes.

Meanwhile, we're starving! Being outlaws, we have to keep moving about, so we can't grow our own vegetables which is what most people do. We have to buy them to make our pottage.

Recipe for Pottage ◊ by Goodwife Delilah Smythe

To a cooking pot halfe fulle of water, adde
meate fisshe or chicken
(whatever thou hast handy)
then adde leakes, onions, chibols*, shallots,
field peas, broad beans (in season)

adde parsley, garlic and hyssop to taste
Leave to fester on the hob for several days.

I'm not saying pottage is to die for, but at least it's a change from venison. We can't buy bread or ale either, so we have to drink water and eat humble pie (which is made from all the bits of deer, like the intestines, that even the dogs turn their noses up at).

* *spring onions.*

Apparently, all the King's ransom money is being kept in huge cash boxes in St Paul's Cathedral. Some of the outlaws said that we ought to nip down to London and nick it.

Robin went doolally! He said, how on earth could we think of such a wicked thing? There were dozens of reasons why such an idea was out of the question (although he could only name four):

1) The money would be heavily guarded
2) We'd never be able to carry it all back
3) We didn't steal from the King
4) If we took the money, King Richard wouldn't be released.

I thought of answering:

1) Fair point
2) We could give it a good go
3) Yes we do – what about all the venison we've scoffed?
4) So what?

But then I thought better of it. As far as Robin is concerned, King Richard can do no wrong.

News of the Wood

25th September 1193

ROBIN HOOD CAPTURED!

The notorious outlaw Robin Hood was captured in St Mary's Church, Nottingham today. The outlaw had gone to the church in disguise, but he was recognised by Brother Jeffrey, a monk from St Mary's Abbey in York who had been robbed of eight hundred pounds by Robin Hood over a year ago.

The monk went immediately to the Sheriff, who hurried to the church with a band of guards. Despite putting up a fierce fight, Robin Hood was captured and thrown in the dungeon of Nottingham Castle.

This is a bit of a poser and no mistake. Little John's been going round crying his eyes out and moaning that it's all his fault. Apparently he told Robin not to go to Nottingham, and Robin said he hadn't been to church in ages and he jolly well would go, so there. They had a row and Little John went off in a sulk. So now Little John is blaming himself for Robin's capture, and Marian's going spare at him for letting Robin get into trouble.

Ah well, I suppose someone will just have to go and rescue the silly idiot.

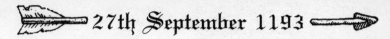

When I said someone would have to go and rescue Robin, I didn't mean me!

Little John and I were lying in wait on the road to London, trying to think what to do, when who should come by but the monk from St Mary's Abbey who'd put the finger on Robin!

As soon as he saw us, he screeched, "I know you! You're Little Jim!"

Little John doesn't like people making fun of his name. He lost his temper a bit.

A letter fell out of the monk's habit. It was addressed to Prince John.

"Well," I said, "we'd better deliver this ourselves, hadn't we?"

27th October 1193

Do my feet ache!

I've just got back from London. We took the monk's letter to Prince John at Westminster. He read it and asked what had happened to the monk? I said he had died suddenly on the road, which was true enough.

Prince John wrote a letter back to the Sheriff.

The Royal Palace
Westminster
11th October 1193

Dear Sheriff,
I hope you are well. Please send me the outlaw
Robin Hood so that I can be very cruel to him.
Yours sincerely,
Prince John

We delivered Prince John's letter to the Sheriff this morning. He wanted to know where the monk was, too.

"Oh," I said, "Prince John was so pleased with him for helping catch Robin Hood, he made him Abbot of Westminster."

News of the Wood

28th October 1193

ROBIN HOOD ESCAPES!

Robin Hood escaped from custody today as the Sheriff of Nottingham was taking him to London on the orders of Prince John. As soon as the prisoner and his escort had left the town, they were set upon by a gang of over one hundred outlaws, who drove off the guards and freed the prisoner. It is understood that two of the outlaws had joined the escort in disguise and gave the signal for the attack. *Me and Little John. Clever, eh?*

The Sheriff of Nottingham was not available for comment as he is having several arrows removed from his seat of office.

Alan A'Dale says that the Sheriff had "an arrow escape". His jokes are worse than his songs!

I hear the Sheriff is going to London tomorrow to explain to Prince John how Robin Hood escaped. I'd give a pound to see their faces when they realise that Little John and I carried all their messages and knew all their plans.

Robin nearly gave the whole thing away, of course. I managed to kick his shin before he could blurt out something like, "Little John! How jolly nice to see you!" which would have been a bit of a giveaway – but he still kept bursting into roars of laughter and winking at me until I was sure the Sheriff would rumble us.

Anyway, he was really pleased to be rescued and gave me a kiss on both cheeks, just as if I was an earl like him.

It's good to have him back, the big soft twit.

```
MICROHARD CHAIN MAIL MESSAGE
From      Basil Count de Money
          (bas@crusade.net)
Date      4 February 1194, 12.33pm
To        len.dusomoney@sherwood.com
Subject   Richard free! (or rather, very
          expensive)
```

Richard was released today! The German
Emperor said, "Thanks for the dosh, *Auf
Wiedersehen*!" (I think that's German for
"buzz off".)

But it nearly didn't happen. Prince John
and Philip of France offered to give the
Emperor a bundle of cash to keep Richard
imprisoned. The Emperor said *"Nein."* John
said he couldn't afford nine bundles of
cash and the Emperor went off muttering
something about *"Englischer Schweinhund"*
and let Richard go.

I wouldn't like to be in John's shoes
when Richard gets hold of him!

Yours, finally homeward bound!

Basil

20th March 1194

WELCOME HOME, KING!

King Richard the Lionheart is back in England! He landed at Sandwich in Kent today with his mother, who delivered his ransom to the Emperor of Germany. He is now heading towards Canterbury Cathedral for a thanksgiving service, and then travels to London. Reports say that Prince John is lying low in France. The King of France is also reported to be very worried.

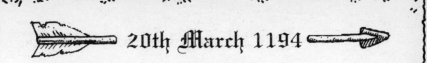

20th March 1194

Marian came dashing through the wood, waving a newspaper in the air.

"Wobin, Wichard has weturned!" she hooted. Here we go, I thought. Richard will want more money, and when he's got it, he'll pack off back to France to teach brother John and King Philip a lesson.

Of course, Marian's mind was on something else. "Wobin," she trilled, "we can get mawwied!"

Robin went all goofy. "Yes bunnikins, we can!"

"Mrs Wobin Hood of the Gweenwood," giggled Marian.

Oh gweat, I thought.

Well, it's been an interesting day!

This morning, I showed Robin the books and said that he needed to do some robbing as he'd got a wedding to pay for. He agreed and went off to find a kind "donor".

He came back with an abbot and a monk. He'd found them wandering through Sherwood. I thought the abbot looked familiar, but I couldn't put my finger on where I'd seen him before.

After we'd feasted (whaddaya know – venison), Robin challenged the abbot to a shooting contest. "If I hit the target, I hit you on the head. If I miss, you hit me!"

Robin was just about to shoot when I sneezed.

He missed.

"Oops," I said. "Bless me!"

The abbot said that Robin could try again, but Robin refused.

"That's wight, wules are wules," said Marian.

"All right then!" said the abbot, rolling up his sleeve. It was then that I noticed how big his muscles were!

As Robin lay dazed on the floor, I thought I'd better give the abbot his bill, before he punched us all and did a runner.

ROBIN'S FOREST BISTRO

2 Vension Specials	£40
Service	£20
RAT*	£20
Total	£80

Have a nice day!
If you have any comments about how we can improve our service, please keep them to yourself.

*Robin Added Tax.

"I'm sorry, I haven't any money," said the abbot.

"Ha," I laughed. "You and everyone else! No one has got any money thanks to King Richard."

The monk stared at me. The abbot said, "And what do you mean by that?"

I took a deep breath:

First of all the King takes most of our money just so he can go off having a good time crusading all over the place, then he stays away for ages, letting his brother take over and take more money off us, and then finally, what little money we've got left is needed for a ransom because he's stupid enough to get himself captured whilst travelling through enemy territory....

As I ran out of breath, I noticed the monk was shaking his head at me. He pulled his hood back. I gawped. It was my cousin Basil!

I stared at the abbot. His face was going as red as his hair.

Red hair?

I looked around. All the outlaws were kneeling down and bowing their heads.

Oops, I thought. That's no abbot, that's the King.

So Richard the Lionheart spent the evening laughing, drinking and feasting with Robin and the outlaws. I spent the evening tied up and hanging upside-down from a tree.

8th April 1194

King Richard stayed for the wedding. It was Robin's idea to have the wedding in Sherwood Forest, but Marian insisted on having another service in Edwinstowe Church (otherwise she wouldn't feel "pwoperly mawwied", she said). Here's one of the wedding photos:

BACK

Alan A'Dale · Hugo Thisaway · Igor Thataway · Rob de Rich · Stan and Dee Liver

Leonard du So Money

George O'Green · Will Stutley · Much the Millers Son · Will Scarlet · The Brides Dad · Maid Marian

FRONT

The reception cost a fortune! I came over all wobbly when I saw the bill, and had to sit down. Robin doesn't care, and nor does Marian. There can't be many girls who can say that the King of England danced at their wedding.

ROW

ck de Loot | Ivan Alibi | Tel Phibbs | Hugh Basham | Alan A 'Dale *

obin Hood | Friar Tuck | King Richard | Little John | Reynold Greenleaf | Right-Hitting Brand

ROW

Again: he nipped round the back and got on twice.

CORONATION 2
He's back! And he's mean!

Richard Plantagenet is
KING OF ENGLAND

To prove it, he's going to be crowned again. The comeback is at Winchester Cathedral. **APRIL 17th** *BE THERE*

What a repeat coronation!

Everyone was there! Dukes, earls, lords, ladies, knights, bishops and *us*!

After Richard had been crowned, he called Robin forward. The King told Robin that he could have his title back and all the lands as well.

Wonderful. No more forest floor!

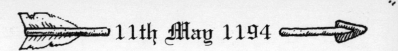

I've had about as much of King Richard the Lionheart as I can take. He stomps about the place yelling orders, laughing one minute, losing his temper the next, and generally being loud. It's enough to give anyone a headache.

The good news is that he's off to France tomorrow to sort out Prince John and King Philip. The bad news is that now Robin is Earl of Huntingdon, he has to go and fight for Richard. Little John, Will Scarlet and some of the other lads are going with him. Cousin Basil's going as well (I thought he'd have more sense than to get involved in another of Richard's "trips").

I'm not going. I've got to sort out Robin's estate. I've got money to collect, accounts to deal with and a proper bed to sleep in.

The rest of Robin's men are all slipping away, back to their farms and villages, and Marian's having hysterics.

It's all very sad.

```
MICROHARD CHAIN MAIL MESSAGE
From      Basil Count de Money
          (bas@alloverfrance.net)
Date      23 July 1194, 7.44pm
To        len.dusomoney@huntingdon. com
Subject French vacation
```

Can you believe it? Richard let John off!
No hot pokers, no prison cell. He just
said, "John, you've been behaving like a
big baby, don't do it again."

We've spent the past couple of months
charging around France, chasing after
Philip's army, but we kept missing them.
Richard swore he'd cut Philip to pieces,
but now he's just agreed a truce with him.
I wish he'd make up his mind!

Yours, as brassed off as a couple of
candlesticks,

Basil

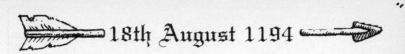
It's been a pleasant few months. No Robin and Marian with their lovey-dovey talk, no awful jokes, no Alan A'Dale, no forest.

I knew it was too good to last!

Marian and I were strolling in the courtyard today when we heard a yell from the sentry up on the battlements. I shouted up and asked him what he could see.

Robin Hood, Robin Hood,
Riding through the glen,
It's Robin Hood, Robin Hood
With his band of men.

I asked him was he taking the mickey or what?

But it really was Robin and the rest of the lads, back from the wars. Richard sent them home to have a rest now he's made peace with King Philip.

Robin was immediately smothered by Marian.

"Oh Wobin, I've missed you!" she said.

"So did the French archers," laughed Robin.

"Oh, give me a cuddle, you gweat gween hunk!"

I staggered away to be sick.

Will Scarlet had his arm in a sling, but Much the Miller's Son was carrying a crossbow that he must have nicked off some Frenchman, and they all seemed pretty chipper.

Let's hope all the fighting's over and we can have a bit of peace at last.

EDITORS' NOTE

The following entries for the years 1195–1198 tell of life at Huntingdon. The diaries are mostly concerned with domestic details. Robin and Marian settled down to run a peaceful household and look after their estates.

The truce between Richard and King Philip soon broke down and the wars in France continued. Between 1196 and 1198, Richard built the greatest castle of the Middle Ages, Château Galliard.

Basil Count de Money continued to keep in touch with his cousin Leonard...

continues...

```
MICROHARD CHAIN MAIL MESSAGE
From      Basil Count de Money
          (bas@alloverfrance.net)
Date      26 March 1199, 11.54pm
To        len.dusomoney@huntingdon. com
Subject   A bolt from the blue
```

It's finally happened! Richard has run out
of luck.

We've been besieging the castle at
Chalus. During the siege, Richard has been
playing the game of "You shoot at me and
I'll dodge the arrow." Usually, Richard's
very good at it. Only this time he wasn't.
The arrow hit him in the top of his
shoulder.

He rode back to his tent and asked me
to pull it out. I tried but it snapped,
leaving the arrow head inside. Two
surgeons tried to get the head out, but
they made a right mess of doing it.

The wound's started to swell and smell.
Things don't look too good...
Yours, as worried as a bull in a
butcher's backyard,
Basil

I read today's newspaper to Robin.

THE LION ROARS NO MORE!

News of the Wood

6th April 1199

King Richard died today in the arms of his mother, Eleanor. He was forty-one and had been King of England for ten years. He had spent only five months of his reign in England and had not visited the country for five years.

The cause of death was an infected wound. Richard had recently been shot by Peter Basilus, a defender at the castle of Chalus.

Richard had no children. His successor is expected to be his brother, John.

In his will Richard gave away a quarter of his wealth to the poor.

"A friend of mine told me it was good to give to the poor," said Richard just before he died.

Organ transplant

Richard's brain and internal organs are to be buried at the Abbey of Charroux. His heart is to be buried at Rouen. What's left of him will be buried in Fontevrault Abbey, where his dad is also buried.

There were tears in Robin's eyes when I finished reading. I had tears in my eyes as well. John is going to be King. That means major trouble.

Marian and I waved Robin off this morning. He's going to France for Richard's funeral. I begged him not to, but I might as well have saved my breath. Robin's always been faithful to Richard (not that Richard ever deserved it, in my opinion).

What worries me is that the minute Robin's back is turned, the Sheriff of Nottingham will take Huntingdon away from him and give it back to that creep Guy of Gisborne.

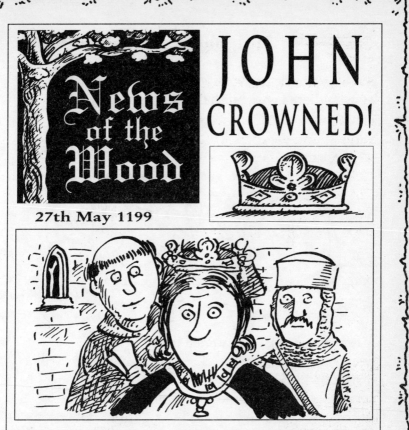

News of the Wood

JOHN CROWNED!

27th May 1199

Prince John became King of England at last today in Westminster Abbey. The new King immediately announced that he was going to reverse all the decisions made by his elder brother Richard. He made Earl Robert of Huntingdon an outlaw, and gave the earldom to Sir Guy of Gisborne.

In his speech to the barons, King John said that he intended to hunt down anybody he didn't like, raise lots of taxes and be particularly nasty to Saxons.

Oh well. Back to the Greenwood.

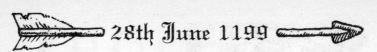

28th June 1199

Robin got back from France a few days ago. He'd have got here faster but he'd had to dodge King John's patrols.

A few of the lads have joined us in the forest. Everyone is trying to be cheerful, saying things will work out all right when a few more of the lads get here, it'll be just like old times, etc – but that's just talk. There's no King Richard to fight for, nobody to come back one day and make everything better. Anyone who joins us now will be an outlaw for life.

The word is that the Sheriff is sniffing around looking for trouble, and so is Guy of Gisborne. Robin's sent Marian to Kirklees Priory. The Prioress is his cousin, and she'll make sure Marian is safe. Marian wasn't keen on the idea, but she could see the sense in it.

"Never mind, Wobin," she said as she left. "One day soon, we shall be weunited!"

I hope so.

News of the Wood

10th August 1199

ROBIN HOOD ROUTED!

The Sheriff of Nottingham led a raid against the outlaw Robin Hood today. The Sheriff attacked the outlaws' base in Sherwood Forest. Many of the outlaws were killed, though Robin Hood himself was not in the camp at the time. Among the prisoners is Robin Hood's lieutenant, Little John.

I got a bang on the head when the fighting began and woke up tied to a tree. Shortly after this, Little John came rushing into the camp, roaring like a madman. He tried to shoot the Sheriff, but his bow broke and he was captured.

Little John told me that he and Robin were out on patrol when they saw a dodgy-looking character wearing a horse skin. Robin said he'd find out what this fellow was up to and sent Little John to fetch reinforcements. On the way home, Little John met Will Scarlet running for his life and found out what had happened at the camp. Being Little John, he decided he'd take on the Sheriff all by himself, which was not only very brave but incredibly stupid.

So there we were, both tied up like rabbits for the pot. The Sheriff was licking his lips and going, "Ho ho ho." It didn't look to me as if he was planning to let us off with a caution.

Then the man in the horse skin showed up.

"Gisborne!" yelled the Sheriff. "Have you killed Robin Hood?"

"I have, my lord," said Gisborne in a husky voice. "His head is in my saddlebag."

I felt a lump in my throat. Poor old Robin. Poor old me!

The Sheriff said, "Oh goody," and went for a rummage.

Gisborne, the vicious swine, asked if he could kill the prisoners. The Sheriff said, "Oh, all right, seeing as it's you."

I was just bracing myself for a knife in the ribs when the man in the horse skin pulled off his hood

(well, it was actually the horse's head, yeuch) and I saw that it wasn't Gisborne. It was Robin! He cut our ropes with a knife, and handed us a bow each.

While Robin was setting us free, the Sheriff was still rummaging in the saddlebag. He pulled Gisborne's head out, and said, "Here, this isn't Robin Hood."

Robin said, "No, *this* is Robin Hood."

And then he shot the Sheriff through the heart. The Sheriff's men took one look and scarpered. Little John and I were bouncing round like kids shouting "bull's-eye!" until we realised Robin was swaying on his feet.

He told us he'd met Sir Guy, killed him, cut off his head and stolen his horse skin as a disguise – but in the fight, Sir Guy had stabbed Robin in the side with his sword.

Robin is bleeding very badly. Little John and I will have to get him some help as soon as we can.

We were wondering what to do with Robin when
Little John fished a leaflet out of his britches pocket.
It said:

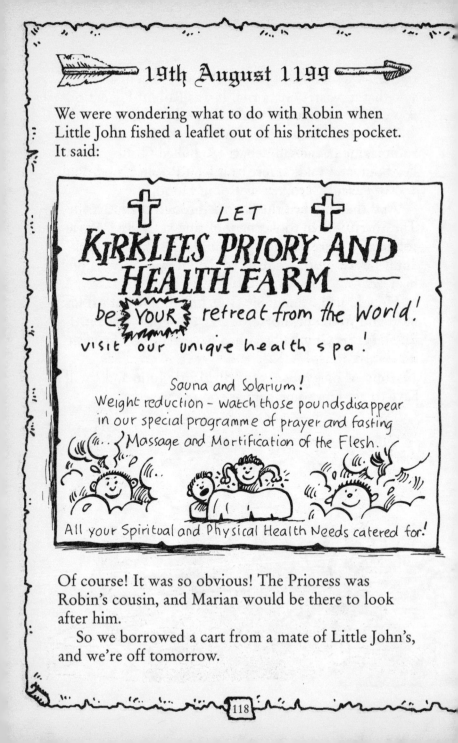

LET

✝ KIRKLEES PRIORY AND HEALTH FARM ✝

be ⚡YOUR⚡ retreat from the World!

visit our unique health spa!

Sauna and Solarium!
Weight reduction - watch those pounds disappear
in our special programme of prayer and fasting
Massage and Mortification of the Flesh.

All your Spiritual and Physical Health Needs catered for!

Of course! It was so obvious! The Prioress was
Robin's cousin, and Marian would be there to look
after him.

So we borrowed a cart from a mate of Little John's,
and we're off tomorrow.

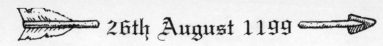

26th August 1199

It's taken us a week to get here – we had to go slowly because Robin's in so much pain.

He looks in a bad way to me, but as soon as we got here the Prioress said he must be bled and that would be ten silver pieces please.

I said, surely he'd lost enough blood already? The Prioress said, oh, thank you for the diagnosis, Mister Bigshot, and just exactly who was the doctor round here, her or me?

I can't say I like the look of the Prioress much – she's got nasty beady little eyes that look right through you. But Marian (as soon as she'd stopped laying into Little John and me for letting Robin get hurt) said of course we must let the Prioress do whatever she thought was right, so that was that.

Robin is dead.

I knew I was right not to trust the Prioress. It turns out she's always been jealous of Robin. Even worse, she was a friend of the Sheriff. So she made a cut in Robin's arm and let his blood drain into a porringer*. What none of us spotted was that the porringer had a hole in it, so we didn't realise how much blood Robin had lost before it was too late. Little John wanted to burn the Priory to the ground, but Robin, weak as he was, still managed to say that he wouldn't let anyone hurt a woman.

* A small bowl.

Robin realised he was dying. As he lay in Marian's arms, he asked for his bow to be brought to him once more. Then he set an arrow to it and aimed out of the window.

With his dying breath, he murmured:

"Wherever this arrow falls, there let me lie."

Actually, he was so weak that his arrow made a sad little arc across the room and stuck in the skirting-board, which would have been an awkward place for a grave. But when we looked out of the window, we saw a nice little clearing among the trees that Robin's shot would probably have reached if he'd had his strength, and we reckoned that was near enough.

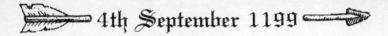

It was Robin's funeral today.

Friar Tuck came and read the service. Will Scarlet was there, and Alan A'Dale, Much, and all the lads who survived the attack on our camp – and Little John and me, of course. The Prioress has been driven out, and Marian has joined the nuns at the Priory. They all came to pay their respects.

We had a marble tombstone made for Robin to show our appreciation. It cost an arm and a leg, but I didn't mind. I've put the cost against death duties!

Alan A'Dale wrote a poem (for once I didn't object) and had carved it on the stone.

> Here, underneath this little stone
> Lies Robert, Earl of Huntingdon.
> No archer ever was so good
> And people called him Robin Hood.
> Such outlaws as he and his men
> Will England never see again.

HISTORICAL NOTE
by R. Celavie, Professor of History
at Trinity College, Basingstoke

This diary does nothing to solve the mystery of Robin Hood. It contains many references to things that did not exist in the twelfth century (e-mail, newspapers, package holidays, etc) and is therefore clearly a forgery.

The origins of the Robin Hood legend remain shrouded in mystery. There may have been an outlaw called Robin Hood who lived in the reign of King Richard the Lionheart. However, there is no real proof of his existence. All we know is that the tales of Robin Hood were so popular by the year 1262 that "Robin Hood" had become a common name for an outlaw. The first mention of "Robert Hod, a fugitive", dates from 1226. So it is likely that over the years there have been many Robin Hoods living as outlaws, and their deeds have been added to the legend.

The fact that there is no record of the Robin Hood who was the enemy of the Sheriff of Nottingham and Prince John does not prove that this man never existed. Governments have always been better at recording their successes than their failures, and John certainly failed to capture Robin Hood.

All we can be sure of is that Robin Hood stands for freedom. Perhaps that is the only existence he has ever had.

But perhaps that is enough.

Order Form

To order direct from the publishers, just make a list of the titles you want and fill in the form below:

Name ....

Address ....

....

....

Send to: Dept 6, HarperCollins Publishers Ltd, Westerhill Road, Bishopbriggs, Glasgow G64 2QT.

Please enclose a cheque or postal order to the value of the cover price, plus:

UK & BFPO: Add £1.00 for the first book, and 25p per copy for each additional book ordered.

Overseas and Eire: Add £2.95 service charge. Books will be sent by surface mail but quotes for airmail despatch will be given on request.

A 24-hour telephone ordering service is available to holders of Visa, MasterCard, Amex or Switch cards on 0141- 772 2281.

Collins
An *Imprint of* HarperCollins*Publishers*